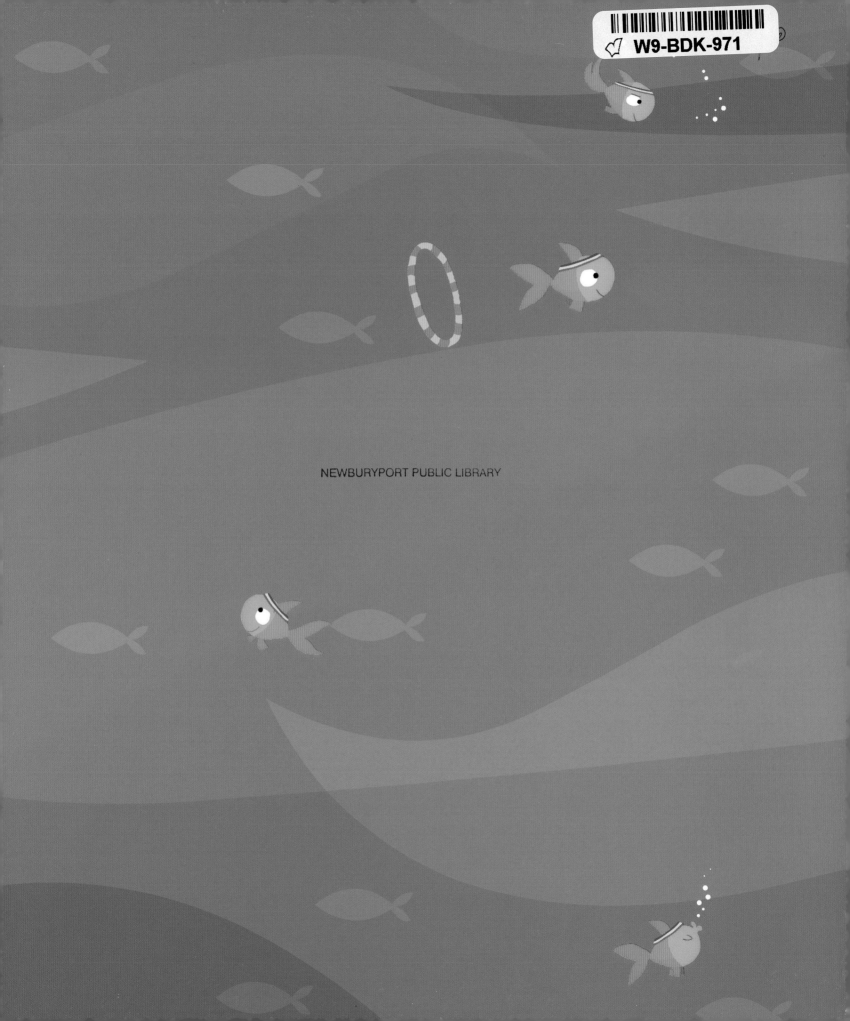

For Bennett, Dylan, Jack & Aiden,
the four "finniest" grands—with glugs
KB

To Kelly—thank you for creating
one AMAZING goldfish!
NZJ

First edition 2020

Library of Congress Catalog Card Number pending
ISBN 978-1-5362-0671-5

20 21 22 23 24 25 LEO 10 9 8 7 6 5 4 3 2 1

Printed in Heshan, Guangdong, China

This book was typeset in Shinn Medium.
The illustrations were created digitally.

Candlewick Press
99 Dover Street
Somerville, Massachusetts 02144

www.candlewick.com

NORMAN
One Amazing Goldfish!

Kelly Bennett

illustrated by Noah Z. Jones

CANDLEWICK PRESS

Norman is
One Amazing Goldfish!

And I want everyone to know it.
That's why I'm taking him to Pet-O-Rama.

GOT A PET?
PET
"O"
RAMA!

PET-O-
RAMA!!

We have our routine all worked out.

First Norman does his tricks:

circles,

then bubbles,

then flips.

And for our big finish, we learned a brand-new tuba song.
"Hit it, Norman!" I say, and begin to play.

Bom ba-bom ba-bom
ba-bom ba-beeeeeee!

Right on cue, Norman starts dancing and singing:

Glug glu-glug glu-glug glu-glug glu-gluuuuuuug!

"Atta-fish, Norman!" I cheer.

"Just wait until everyone sees you! You'll be famous!"

On Pet-O-Rama day, I wake up extra early.

I don't want to admit it, but I am sort of nervous.

Not Norman. He gobbles every bite of his breakfast.

The Pet-O-Rama line is super long.

There are dogs, cats, birds, rabbits, snakes, and lots of other animals.

Most of the kids are wearing costumes. So are their pets.

I look at Norman. His orange scales glisten.

"You're so sparkly, you don't need a costume, do you, Norman?"

He shoots me a high-fin.

PET
-O-
RAMA

Sign up
Here →

Once we're signed up, Norman and I go into the gym.
Right away we spot Ben and Dylan with their dog, Mustard.
"*Hi-yah!* Mustard does karate," Dylan says. "What does your fish do?"

"Lots of tricks," I say.

"Hey, Fish!" Ben calls. "Show us a trick."

Norman doesn't move. Not even a fin flutters.

Dylan and Ben laugh.
"Pet-O-Rama is for good pets," says Ben.
"Not fish."

WELCOME TO...
Pet-O-Rama

"Norman is amazing," I tell them.
"You'll see!"

One by one by one, the judges call pets onto the stage.
All the pets look good, and many do tricks.
But not any better than Norman's.

"Just wait until they see our act," I whisper.
"We'll show 'em, won't we?"

Norman spits a mouthful of gravel.

When our number is called, I carry Norman onto the stage.
The gym looks really big . . . and crowded.
That nervous feeling is back again, big-time.
I glance over at Norman. Under the stage lights, his scales
and fins *are* as sparkly as any costume. Just looking
at him makes me feel better. I take a deep breath.

"Introducing Norman,

One Amazing Goldfish!"

I announce.

"For our first trick, circles!"
Just as we practiced,
I circle my finger.
In the wings, a poodle
in a tutu twirls.

Not Norman.

"My mistake," I say, trying
hard to keep my voice steady.
"Ready, set, bubbles!"

"Bubbles!" a parrot squawks.
Not Norman.
He doesn't blow even
one teensy blip.

"Come on, Norman. This is an easy one. How's about a flip?
One, two, three—"
My hands are shaking so hard, I barely manage a snap.
"UP!"

Norman hides behind his plant.

I can feel everyone watching, waiting . . .
I give Norman a look. A hard look.
His fins and flippers are quivering like crazy.

That's when it hits me: Norman isn't being stubborn.
He has stage fright, too.

Oh, no! Poor Norman!

"Don't be scared," I whisper. "Ignore them and watch me.
Let's do this together, Norman. Just like at home, OK?"
I take out my tuba. "Hit it, Norman!" I call.
Then I close my eyes and give it my best.

Bom ba-bom ba-bom
ba-bom *ba-beeeeeee!*

I'm starting in on the second section when Ben and Dylan shout,

"Hey, everybody! Look!"

When I open my eyes, the first thing I see is . . .

Norman!

He isn't lying on the bottom of his fishbowl.
He isn't hiding behind his plant, either.

Norman is flip-flop-wiggle-wag dancing like crazy.
And singing!

*Glug glu-glug glu-glug
glu-glug glu-gluuuuuuug!*

Then Norman performs every trick perfectly—
just as we practiced.

"Atta-fish, Norman!" I cheer.

The Pet-O-Rama judges give Norman a prize.

It's like I always say: Norman is

One Amazing Goldfish!